Sonata

By Jackie Kay

Trumpet

Why Don't You Stop Talking

Wish I Was Here

Jackie Kay

Sonata

PICADOR SHOTS

First published 2006 by Picador
an imprint of Pan Macmillan Ltd
Pan Macmillan, 20 New Wharf Road, London N1 9RR
Basingstoke and Oxford
Associated companies throughout the world
www.panmacmillan.com

ISBN-13: 978-0-330-44576-4
ISBN-10: 0-330-44576-6

1 3 5 7 9 8 6 4 2

A CIP catalogue record for this book is available from
the British Library.

Typeset by Intype Libra Ltd
Printed and bound in Great Britain by
Mackays of Chatham plc, Chatham, Kent

PERPHAPS ALL NIGHT TRAINS HAVE this air of the confessional, if two people find themselves in the right carriage, sleepless, watching small stations pass through them like waking dreams. I must have been watching you for a very long time, watching you without appearing to be interested in you at all. I knew we had a long night ahead of us; we had time. And I knew as soon as you opened your mouth that you had a story to tell and that your story would stretch across this troubled country of mine. It was a slow winter. Our journey through X and X and X had a surreal quality to it, as if we would never get to our destination, as if we would spend our lives on this night train, seeing the deep snow glow a little in the dark, the beautiful old lettering of some of our stations light up for a minute and then be gone.

I was staring into the night thinking that no one ever fathoms the dark. The dark is like a mirror. I could see only shapes in the night. I couldn't make them out.

You paused before you mentioned that this love you talked on and on about through the snow and through the small stations of X and X and X, through the thick, conspiratorial darkness, was a woman, and when you mentioned this you looked down into your furs and then looked quietly up again to see my expression. Your lashes blurred at the edges and you blinked prettily, as if you were saying, Are you surprised at this, that here I am this very pretty woman, and here this great love of mine is also a woman? They have an expression I heard used in England quite recently which made me laugh. (I have a loud laugh that is perhaps off-putting. I often try to dim it down.) The expression was *get over yourself*. I think this a good one for many reasons; perhaps all of the problems of the world are to do with the fact that we simply cannot, any of us, anywhere, get over ourselves.

English is not my language and it is not yours; so we could say, we shared English for the night as well. There is a certain camaraderie to be had from sharing a language that belongs to neither of you. You search for the right word; you appreciate what the other finds. The language becomes a kind of a dance; you take one step, I take the other. We both pronounce English differently, we emphasize the wrong part of a word just like beginners in Russian often don't get the sounds right. They never manage the B pronounced like the v of void or X close to the ch sound in the Scottish loch. Sometimes we forget perfectly ordinary words.

You say to me, 'How do you call this green stuff?' and it takes me ten minutes to work out you mean grass.

Let me describe you because you are a woman who likes listening to descriptions of herself. How do I know this? I don't know. Only that I know it. You will smile prettily and your eyes will shine with self-delight. I have met women like you before.

You have very dark eyes, that widen when something surprises you. You are demure. You have long eyelashes. You have beautiful bone structure. You look like a great beauty, like an actress. You have those kind of looks that makes a stranger think they already know you because your beauty is classic. It is known. What is not known are your thoughts. Who ever heard the tormented thoughts of the great beauty? You have thick dark hair. You are wearing dark red lipstick. You are wearing a fur coat. Something in your expression tells me

4

you have recently been having not a good time of it. I don't know what. But as soon as you opened your mouth, I knew that you wouldn't be able to stop, that you would be forced to tell me everything. And I would have to find some way to absolve you. We know things without knowing them.

You knew that your jealousy was a form of craziness, yet you walked towards it. You walked towards it in the pitch dark when all of your intelligence was saying stop. And so, how was it the poet put it? 'The heart that can no longer | Love passionately, must with fury hate.'

When I looked back on that journey with you, I knew I would be able to remember the exact moment your story began because I had been watching you, waiting for it to come. Strangers on the train can be so very intimate; this is true, is it not? We shared that night together and we will never meet again and yet,

I don't want to sound melodramatic, for goodness' sake, I am a little pedantic, and the pedant hates melodrama, but it might not be an exaggeration to say that I felt something towards you that night like love. That journey will stay with me as proof that I am capable of profound intimacy. And yet I knew if I took your number that I would break the spell, that we could not ever repeat it. I think it was different for you than for me. I know you better than you know me. Isn't this always the way in relationships, that one person knows the other better?

Here is how you started. You leaned forward to me and you said, and it was a typical question but it didn't put me off, 'Do you know how long it will be before we reach X?' You spoke right away in English. I said, 'I'm not sure, the train seems to be running behind schedule, but it is so difficult to tell in the night.' You sighed. You were cold. I offered you my scarf and you took it, wrapping it round your neck. I cannot say what pleasure that gave me, watching you, such a great beauty, take my green scarf and wrap it round your neck. If I had known you better I might have asked you to do it again.

You sighed again and hugged yourself. Then you said, 'Do you think if you tell somebody something you still do not believe yourself, that it would help you to believe it?' I nodded. I was uncertain I wanted to hear what you clearly wanted to tell me. Part of me was enjoying sitting opposite you, making you up to myself. I wasn't sure I wanted you to come suddenly alive, to do your own thing. But I nodded because we were two people in the same carriage on a long night journey through the snow and what kind of human being would I be if I could simply not bear to listen? What is the cost of listening, do you think? And why are some people what they call good listeners and other people talkers? And how come talkers never get to be good? I wondered if being a good listener was really such a virtue. I am a terrible cynic because I have been betrayed so many times. Yet I am somebody who is a good listener.

During these hours of our journey, I got up a few times and fetched us a glass of tea from the buffet car. Once we had a vodka at three in the morning. That was the best potato vodka of my life shared with you while you shared your life with me. During your story, I interrupted little except to make the odd observation. You needed my full attention. Nobody has needed my attention like that before, ever. It was, how do they say, *full on*.

We were two women who lived very happily together in an apartment in the old part of town. We were discreet about our relationship. Many people mistook us for sisters because we were both good-looking and svelte, slim, and because we loved each other so much something about us became the same, the same. We dressed similarly. We shared our undergarments. We held each other all night long. At first we had sex – lots and lots of sex, no, and then we had no sex, yes? It was as if we became too . . . much, too intimate to have it, too close to each other's skin. Not enough to separate us, mmmmmnnh? We became like family, each other's mother and father and sister. I don't know. Explain to me how this happens. How you can go from ripping each other's clothes off to a kiss like this?

You purse your lips and kiss the cold night air.

And why this is. Is it because each of us is frightened of closeness sexually, and can only maintain it for a short period? I don't know. It's complex, no?

We worked at similar jobs. We loved our work and we could share that totally. We were a little competitive but we never admit this to each other. This was another problem, that we were rivals like siblings can be rivals in the most awful way, whilst pretending to be each other's, how do you say, support, leaning on each other? We had to rely on each other a lot. There were not many people that we knew in Zagreb like us. I could have died for her. I could have put my hand beside my heart and promised to be with her when she was old – even when her skin was wrinkled and her teeth were not her own any more. Supposing she had been taken ill? I could have put my hand beside my heart and sworn to look after her, to take a cold flannel to her hot forehead, to wash her feet, to change her sheets. I often imagined this, is that strange, don't you think? I don't know why. But I imagined looking after her if she was ill. In my head maybe it was a test of love, because there are things about illness which I find revolting.

And it is strange now to look back on that

time and to see how certain I felt about the future, about becoming an old woman, with her. I could have bet good money in the casino that we would be being together forever. Anything else was an outrage. Of course occasionally we would have arguments and at those times we would get very hard and upset and both of our hearts would hurt. But we never went to sleep without making things a little better. Usually it was with me saying sorry, sorry, sorry, yes? Usually at least three times to make it work properly – like a spell.

And then one morning, I got up and smiled at her and kissed her cheek and she got up out of bed very quickly. She said she had to hurry and that she was late for work and that was the last time I ever kissed her cheek in the morning. That night she came home with things from the delicatessen and left me some cheese, some chorizo, an artichoke, some olives, and a large red tomato on a white plate and said she was taking hers to her study to continue working. I ate the artichoke heart, which wasn't very tasteful, then threw the rest in the bin. It was so unusual for us not to eat together. I felt sick in the stomach.

At this point an old man came into our carriage and sat down. He was wearing a thick coat and a big fur hat. He took off his hat and nodded to us and lit his pipe. Then he said in my language, 'A very cold night, is it not? The train is running late. So much snow on the tracks.' I spoke with him a little. I was impatient to get back to you. I knew you might not speak now. 'How far are you going?' I asked him. He said he was only going as far as X. I looked at you and you looked at me back as if to say, Of course I can wait till X. You got up and went to the toilet and I missed you while you were gone. I had such a strong sense of our time being so short that I didn't want a single moment of it wasted. I never experienced this before. Actually quite the opposite. I am usually one of those people who discourages the train conversation, where are you going, who to see, for how long, etc. I never have interesting answers for a start. I am not usually visiting anybody. Of course I am a hopeless neurotic and I say this only for you to realize how unusual it was, for me at least, to be so engrossed, so compelled, so open to you.

When you came back, I noticed that you had freshened up your hair, and it was now sitting on top of your head. You had redone your red lipstick. You looked pale and impatient. You looked vampire pale; your white face made your red lipstick all the more red.

The old man took you in and smiled at you. I could see that he was charmed by your beauty. The beautiful have so much easier a time of it than the ugly, don't you think? They get smiled at the whole time. Strangers offer them things. People notice the beautiful; the beautiful are constantly acknowledged. They get service at the drop of a hat, faster service in bars and restaurants than the ugly. If they are crossing a road, cars stop for them quicker. It is true, but only the ugly would notice it. You were used to being noticed. I suddenly realized, before you even told me the next part of your story, that what had cut you was not the betrayal, but the fact that you were used to being noticed. You were used to getting all of her attention. You were one of those people in the world who is good at getting attention. Some don't need it and some crave it and some go to childish lengths to procure it. This was it, surely, the person who had given you all of her attention for thirteen years suddenly turned off the light and you could not see your beautiful face any more. You needed her to give you your own reflection, I think? It was like you were travelling on a train in the dark.

The old man closed his eyes; then you closed

your eyes; then I closed mine. And the three of us shared forty winks. Then the train shuddered into X and the old man rubbed his eyes. He climbed the steep steps onto the platform and I bent down and handed him his old, battered case. He thanked me warmly but looked at you. The beauty. Even though you didn't lift a beautiful finger to help the old man. Such is life. You see. I am used to the ways of it.

A younger man put his head through our carriage door and my heart sank. But he didn't like the trail of pipe tobacco the old man had left. You watched him sniff the air and then walk on. I felt relief. So did you. I could see it on your face, it swept across the plane of your high cheeks. I sat down opposite you. Your head was leaning against the window. You stared out at the snow for some time. The train was still stationary and we could see the snow better, lit up by the lights in the station. It shone with the promise of oblivion. You got out your silver cigarette case and took a cigarette from it. You offered one to me. I shook my head but slipped your silver lighter out of your hand, just as you were about to light your cigarette, and lit it for you myself. You breathed your smoke in deeply and exhaled, blowing a thin, quick line of smoke out of the corner of your mouth. You held the cigarette poised in your hand. I thought perhaps that you were not going to tell me any more. Your face looked troubled by too many thoughts. The train started up again, its engine coughing and spluttering in the cold. It juddered and for a moment it sounded like the engine was going to fail completely. Then it seemed to will itself into movement and we took off again. It got darker and darker inside our carriage.

That night I put the chorizo and cheese in the bin, I heard her playing the piano in our living room. We had a beautiful baby grand piano that had been lifted into our apartment through the sash windows with a crane. The day it arrived, all the neighbours gathered around in the street outside and watched it being pulled up into our front room like a great black bird. It was such a special day. Everyone out in the street with their mouths open, yes, nobody spoke a single word, until the piano was safe and then people spontaneously clapped, as if we were all at the opera.

Her playing sounded different. It sounded out of control. She played a piece I had heard her play before, the Kreutzer Sonata, but this time she played it as if the demon were in her fingers. It made me feel fearful just to listen to it. It made me think of white dogs in the snow, of red meat. It made me think that something violent was going to happen to my life. I opened the door a little and watched her at the piano. I am not exaggerating. No, it is not too much to say she looked possessed, yes? She did not look well. Her long hair was hanging over her face. She usually put it up to play. Her face had such a strong look of concentration, she looked vicious. Not at all pretty any more. She was talking to herself fiercely as she played, counting, totally involved in the music. If a bomb had exploded at the end of the street she would have sat playing amongst the rubble. The skin on her face was tight with ambition. I looked down horrified at her foot, her foot pressing on the pedal of the piano with such precision, such poise, in her black leather shoes. Even the instep of her foot was rigidly tense, ready to pounce. It was as if the piano, which used to be a source of leisure and pleasure, had now become her prey. I closed the door quietly and went to bed early with my book. Can you believe it but I was rereading *Crime and Punishment*? Even at night that summer it was too hot. The heat trapped you in your own home.

'This summer gone?' I interrupted her to ask.

Yes, this summer gone. Very humid. No breeze. No air. Our apartment was stifling, stuffy. I could feel the desire coming off her. I could feel it. It was revolting. I got out our fan and plugged it in. I could still feel her heat even as I imagined the fan lifting the sheets of music, and making them flutter, as if they were playing on their own. The music got in my head. I could not concentrate for it. It became the music of the end of our relationship, the music of our finale. I will never be able to listen to it again as long as I live. What a thing it is to have music that plays your terrible thoughts. I imagined that one piece could drive more delicate women than myself to insanity.

'Goodness,' I said, 'what a pity. I know that piece. It is a wonderful piece of music. Do you not think we should listen more objectively when we listen to music?'

'Perhaps,' you said, and looked out of the window, considering my question. 'Perhaps,' you said again, as if you actually might like to impress me. You rubbed your shoulders, cold still, and tightened my scarf around your neck. I could see your breath in the carriage. The heating was not working properly. I was annoyed at myself for interrupting you. You seemed to have left me to go back into your own world. Very still moments passed between us as the train slid through the middle of my country. I looked out of the window and thought how the near dark and the far away dark are different colours. There was a half-moon in the sky. It had a blood-red glow around it. It looked as if it had been sliced cleanly down the middle with a butcher's knife.

She told me she was going to be playing the Kreutzer Sonata with Isadora, this new friend of hers, yes. She was excited because she said they had been asked to play at a charity concert. Am I stupid? Did she think I don't see what is laid before my eyes to see? Is she pretty, this Isadora? I asked her one night playing with her hair. She took my hand away. Don't do this, she said, it is irritating. You see it had got so crazy she didn't like my touch? Maybe, she said. Her eyes were shining with new light. She didn't even try and hide from me. So I asked her outright. I said, Are you in love with her? Have you fallen for her?

She looked completely shocked; actually she looked appalled. She said, Of course not. Don't be so silly. She is a friend and a fellow musician. I like how she plays the violin. You like how she plays the violin, I echoed because it sounded obscene to me. Yes, she repeated, very innocently, Yes, yes. I like how she plays the violin. It is that simple. She inspires me. I can learn a lot from her. She is really very good. Her timing is superb. Well, but now she was giving me too much detail. Yes, but, I said again. And is she pretty? Well, her looks are not the kind of looks I usually like, she said. She is too tall, blonde. She is not my type. I suppose to others she is pretty. And this did not console me, because she said *usually*. Looking back on it, all that I can think is that I knew before she knew. Perhaps, and this thought is horrible to me, perhaps I even opened her eyes to it by asking that question. Perhaps if I had never asked that question she would have never discovered it?

Anyway, I suppose I believed her that hot night. I told myself that this concert was very important to her and I must stop being so demanding. I tried to support her. I cooked her special little meals. But she would not eat them. I bought good red wine, but she only sipped at it. I bought her a new top, but she thought it didn't suit her. I tried everything. It was like she had fallen sick to me. She so much wanted to do her own thing that anything associated with me was to be pushed away. Like this.

You pushed violently in front of yourself.

I felt like I lived in a small apartment in the old part of town with a cold stranger now. My love, who used to spend every minute with me, was now shutting me out. She had somebody else who made her sparkle and shine. Even if she didn't know it. I knew it. I knew it. And so the day came when I could stand it no longer.

At this point our train pulled into X. Three young men wearing suits and carrying briefcases got into our carriage. They nodded at us. I could see that they thought we were together, maybe friends because of the way they nodded at us as if we were one, not two. I liked that. It made me feel I belonged to somebody for even a short while. On that train journey across our country when our country was suffering all sorts of troubles and when this group were fighting that group, and nobody ever felt completely safe, not even at the opera or the theatre, especially not at the opera or the theatre, I thought to myself, it is possible to feel safe and contained by a stranger in a carriage on a train.

You rolled your eyes when the men came in. You looked at your watch. We still had three hours to go before we reached X. You closed your eyes. I worried that you would fall into a deep sleep and wake up only when we arrived. You looked so tired. You looked as if your story was taking it out of you. I was already considering giving you my number and saying something casual like, 'If you would like to finish telling me your story some other time, you could call me, and we could have a vodka or a grappa or a coffee or whatever . . .' Or something like, 'I have enjoyed being with you on this train so much. I have never had a lover for longer than a year but I think you are beautiful. I understand you completely. Will you meet me again?' Or something like, 'It was meant that we should be in this same carriage. We were meant to meet. You were meant to tell me this story. It is fate. What are we going to do next?' But I am a good listener and not a talker. In the dimming light of our carriage, I noticed your mouth, how full and sensuous it looked as you slept, how your bottom lip was slightly parted from your top one.

The men were men from Moscow and were obviously businessmen. They were talking about money. I never understand talk about money so I simply let the conversation fly over my head. The tall, handsome man's mobile went off in his pocket. He answered, talked for a bit, then I heard him say, 'That's the deal, take it or leave it. I don't know how many times I have to say this!' When he put down the phone, he shook his head, in a temper. 'It was my wife,' he said. 'We are in the middle of an acrimonious divorce.' The shorter man said, 'She rings you up in the middle of the night?'

'Oh yes. She specializes in the middle of the night. The sooner we settle it all the better. It is doing my head in.'

'There's a lot of money in divorce these days. Divorce is big business. It didn't used to be,' the third man said thoughtfully. His hair was black and greased down and he had a rather unappealing centre parting.

You shifted in your seat and snuggled into the side of the carriage. I wondered how my language sounded to you, how much of it you understood. 'Friends of mine from New York paid a lawyer a massive amount in a costly, bitter divorce. They even went to court over their dog, who should get custody of the dog, can you believe that?' the centre-parting man said.

'We don't have a dog or children,' the handsome man said. 'Our problem is we never had enough to share. In the end we just had absolutely nothing in common: zilch.'

I shifted in my seat and looked at you. You had opened your eyes and were staring out of the window again. And then the train pulled into X and the three men got out. They had taken with them half an hour of my story. My eyes burnt holes into their backs. At this point, I still had no idea, absolutely no idea how far your story was going to go. I just knew that you had me hooked, perhaps for my own private reasons.

I was tired. My eyes felt sore from looking into the dark and trying to fathom it. Your voice was now inside my head. It seemed to go with the snow and the dark, your deep, husky, smoker's voice. You halted often, straining to use a language that was not natural for you. This I found sexy, the stopping and the starting. Your voice was like the train. Whenever I go on that same journey again, I think I can hear it under the sound of the wheels on the tracks. It is the particular rhythm of somebody who is not speaking in their mother tongue, though both of us are more fluent in English perhaps than some that live there. I have a friend in London. These days when I ring him to ask him what he is doing he says, 'Just chilling,' and it is so annoying because he rarely says more than that. Perhaps he no longer welcomes my calls. The train is still stationary. I notice you only ever start talking when it moves off, as if you need the sound of the engine or the movement to tell your story. You looked at me and arched your eyebrows and looked at your watch again. Something had changed in the way you told your story now; you seemed reluctant to get back to it, as if you couldn't face it any longer. You gave me the impression that you might just abandon it altogether and fall as silent as the faithful snow outside.

During this period I actually feel as if some

part of myself has been banished to another part of the world. I feel as if I cannot live my life to the full and feel everything I am capable of feeling unless I have this love. The pleasure goes from me; the delight goes. Nothing means anything. I am dulled at my edges. I have a weight across my chest that is as heavy and as surprisingly soft as a snake. I am sure that the weight is the weight of my broken heart. Two pieces of heart weigh more than one. I feel for the first time in my life that life and love are the same thing; without love you have no life. She feels for the first time that passion and life are the same thing. I see it on her cheeks, in her eyes, in the way she moves, in the fact she starts to go on a diet, and in the way she grows her hair and in the different clothes she buys. If she cannot see it, she is a fool. But I see it. But I have no proof. Some part of me says to myself, You don't want to find such proof. But the other part says, Prove that she is a liar. And so

I go hunting for the truth. And this is the how do you say it, when the road goes like this.

You join your wrists together and hold your beautiful hands apart.

'The fork in the road?' I say.

There is another expression I like better than this one.

'The crossroad?' I say.

Exactly. Yes. The crossroad. This is when I could have gone another way but I didn't. And I know it in my own head. I say, Don't do this. You are the one that will pick up the bill for this. Leave her to have her little excitement, she will come back to you when she is finished because you know her like nobody else. You love her like nobody else. Let her have her silly bit of adolescent passion. She has bought for herself some very silly clothes. Not her. They just do not suit her style. I say all this to myself, I talk to myself in a heavily emphasized way. I have lost all my subtlety, all my dignity, all my grace. My head gives me no peace. How can she do this. How can she become this stranger. Has she forgotten herself. Has she forgotten everything we had. Did we ever have what I thought we had and so on. It is non-stop. It follows me everywhere, my own voice like a dog, like a thin dog looking for where it buried the bone. It goes to sleep with me. It wakes up with me. I am raging. I am lost. I look at her sleeping in these days. She sleeps the night away till she can wake and be with her love. She is closed to me even in her sleep.

And so I open up the drawer where I know she keeps her special things and in that drawer what do you suppose I find?

At this point the guard comes in to inspect our tickets. I never understand why a ticket needs to be inspected more than once on the journey. He looks at you closely as he takes your ticket as if he recognizes you, as if he thinks you are a great actress. You put your ticket away in your purse and smile tightly at him. He nods. You nod back. He is a cursory guard; someone who would like to have even more power, I suspect, than his job allows, someone who would really like to put the fear of God into people. He examines me, suspiciously, as if I have cheated him out of something. He takes my ticket and looks at it for a long time. I wonder if there is something wrong with my ticket. He says, 'So you are travelling all the way to X? It is a long journey.' 'Yes,' I say, stumped for anything more to say. 'It is.' The guard nods silently and goes on his way.

I find nothing. I don't know what I expected to find, evidence of some kind, but there are no love letters there, no photographs, no bits of paper with telephone numbers on them, nothing. And yet still, I know it. I know it in my bones. This jealousy is already singing its mean little song to me, like a childhood taunt. I am reduced by it. By day I feel myself grow small.

I look in the mirror and my skin looks dull. The thoughts in my head are not so interesting any more because I have no one to share them with. I try to do certain pathetic things to make myself feel better. I wear high heels because this woman is tall. I have my hair shaped by a very expensive hairdresser. And though she notices some of these things, she seems not at all interested in me any more. She looks at me and sometimes says, 'Your hair is nice,' or some such compliment but she cares nothing, nothing. She speaks like an automaton now. Her mind is far away. I feel how distant she is when she is standing close to me. She could be on the other side of the mountain. There is a mountain air that comes off her radiant cheeks, a fresh, scented air as if she has been to some special place that I have not; even when we have both spent the whole day together, I feel this. The truth is she has an interior life without me, when she used to share the thoughts inside her head. I can feel it, this inside-life that she has. It always places me far away on the outside. It makes me lonely. It makes me, how do you say it, nostalgic for my own past. It makes me homesick while I am still at home.

One time she comes home with this look on her face. How shall I call that look? A certain smugness. I say to her, 'We never make love any more, why don't we?' And she says, 'It has been such a long time that we can't just rush into it. We need to take our time.' 'Take our time?' I say. 'It has been years.' But conversations such as that always pass with no satisfactory outcome. Somehow she just slips out or under them and before I know it we are talking about something else.

You get your cigarettes out and light one and blow out the smoke. Though I have never smoked myself, I don't mind it when you do. You only notice your ash when it becomes quite long, you catch it in the nick of time and flick it into the ashtray at the side of your seat. You manage to look attractive doing this. I can hardly believe what I am hearing. I have never spoken to a more perfect creature. You are beautiful – beautiful and tormented and intelligent and sensitive. It is incomprehensible that someone should not desire you. Goodness, they should be so lucky. I want to lean towards you and kiss your cheek but of course someone like you would never look at someone like me. I am not good-looking enough. I am clumsy, big-boned. Of course I have fine tastes, but having fine tastes is of no use to one if one is big-boned. At the end of the day you still have a large hand around a dainty teacup and it is off-putting, it is not a big draw.

And what is more from the way that you are telling me this story, I can tell that you would not even consider finding me attractive. Perhaps jealousy is not at all what one feels for somebody else, perhaps jealousy is all about what one feels for oneself. Even the beautiful are fragile, I take comfort from this. Perhaps the beautiful are even more fragile because they are beautiful. Perhaps the ugly are less breakable, tougher, happier to be loved at all. We break the world up into opposing groups the whole time, the rich and the poor, the young and the old, the black and the white, men and women, but actually as far as I can see the most neglected difference is between the beautiful and the ugly. The ugly have no rights. They don't even feel the right to be loved. They feel grateful for the simplest of kindnesses, such as someone saying thank you or please or someone holding a door open. Actually we feel grateful to be spoken to, to be taken seriously. You look out of the window. You have lapsed into one of your small silences. I look out of the window too. I cannot believe how endless the snow is during our winters, how implacably there it is, as if it will never, ever melt. The land underneath the thick snow is a secret, a secret months old.

We still slept in the same bed together during this time. I didn't sleep so well any more. I counselled the dark. Sometimes she fell thickly asleep only to wake me up as she laughed and giggled like a maniac in her sleep. When I heard that laughter I knew for definite she was in love. I asked my doctor. She said, Laughing in one's sleep is a sign of being in love. It scared the living daylights out of me. The next morning, I said to her, You were laughing in your sleep. And she looked undressed by me. Then she said, Oh for goodness' sake, leave me alone. Give me some peace. I am tired of being watched. You are making me feel jumpy in my own house. Stop watching my every move or you will finish us off! Watching your every move? I said. What nonsense. You were laughing loudly, hysterically in your sleep. Like this. Hee Heee Heeeee, Ha Ha Ha! You woke me up. That is all. I am not sitting awake watching you sleep, for goodness' sake. You woke me up! Yes, yes, yes, she said. But still, you know what I mean. It is not just then. It is all the time. You are constantly watching me. I feel it.

I am not, I said to her – though of course there was a little truth in what she was saying – I am merely noticing all these sudden changes in you. How can I not notice when they feel like such a rejection?

Oh, stop going on about rejection, she said. It is not sexy. It is so boring. No wonder people that rant on about being rejected get rejected. Leave me alone. Give me some peace.

I wondered if she was being so horrible to me because she felt guilty about betraying me. Or if she just didn't like me any more. She made me feel so disliked. Actually, I felt she was contemptuous of me. She had gone from thinking I was the most important person in her life to treating me like an annoying little cousin that has been sent from Constanta to stay the summer in Bucharest, some little runny-nosed child. Not me. She was not seeing me any more. She had some other impression of me in her head and I couldn't correct it. I couldn't get to what it was. I kept wanting to say, Anna, this is me. This is me, your love. How can you forget me so quickly? How can you cast me in this role?

A thought occurred to me as she was talking. It struck me with force. I could tell that she was a private person, that she was not used to telling strangers her intimate business, so why had she picked me? That was the first thought and the second thought was, given that her confidence had been so diminished by this raging jealousy, how come she felt more than confident to tell me the whole story, without once ever saying, even out of politeness, am I boring you, is this going on too long, are you still interested in my story or even, do you believe me? What gave her the right to tell the story to me in such painstaking detail; what made her think it was interesting to me? Did she see me and suspect that I had similar tendencies? Certain parts of her story did not tally. I did not believe she had gone and asked her doctor about the laughter in the sleep. I excused myself for a moment and told her I had to go to the bathroom. I went to the bathroom and took a good look at myself in the mirror. What had I had by way of lovers? How was I qualified to even understand the complexities that I was hearing? What if her entire story was made up and she had picked me to make a fool of me? Did I believe her every word? Did it matter what I believed? I washed my face with cold water and combed my hair. The train had just pulled into X. I got off the train and went to the buffet on the platform. I bought us both a glass of tea. I came back, handed her the glass of tea, which she took in a distracted way, not noticing really what I was giving her. I felt myself grow a little impatient with her. Yes, yes, I know – the traumatized are monstrously self-obsessed. Whatever she has done has so shocked her that she cannot come out of herself to even notice a stranger bringing her a glass of lemon tea. What do I owe this stranger? I owe her precisely nothing. I have already given her too much. I have listened for nearly six hours now. I have bought her a very good vodka, and two glasses of tea. What is the matter with me? Am I so flattered by the attentions of a pretty woman that I will do anything? If I asked her to close her eyes and describe me, I would not be surprised if she could not manage it. In a way, she is talking to the dark. In a way, I am her mirror.

You look straight at me for a second as if contemplating me. You look as if you are read-ing my thoughts. I feel a little unnerved by the frankness of your stare. Then you say quietly, in your deep, sexy voice, 'Thank you for the tea.' The smile on my face is perhaps too large. I say, 'Oh, it is nothing. You are very welcome.'

So one day I thought to myself: enough, I am fearing this woman I have never seen. I am making things up to myself. If only I could see her, then I would know for sure. That evening – a rare evening of calm between us, something had settled and it seemed as if we could live on with this familiarity, this thing that was not passion any more, but was still caring – I suggested something. I knew she didn't want to leave me. Otherwise, she would have left already, no? I knew I was her security. She still needed me. She needed to come home to our home and sleep in our bed and play her piano. She was too much of a coward to simply say, I am sorry I have fallen in love. We must divide. And for my part, though I was not contented, I thought, I cannot imagine my life without her. Anna is my life. I must try and adapt and cope with her changes and maybe good things will come of these changes. Maybe somebody somewhere will reward me for my perseverance.

So I said to her that night, Perhaps we should have a few friends around and you should practise your sonata with Isadora and they can hear you play? It would be a dress rehearsal, no? We could have some food, some wine, some music. It has been so long since we had company. She looked at me a little suspiciously at first as if trying to find some other motive. Then her face broke into a smile and she kissed me for the first time in ages on my cheek.

You touch your cheek quite theatrically.

Well, thank you, Esther, she said. I think it is a good idea.

A few weeks later we had ten friends round. I had ordered and prepared the food and tidied our apartment, which was always very tidy in any case. Anna put on a beautiful new dark red dress and she looked quite lovely. I felt a stab of desire for her just like I had in the beginning of our love. Her cheeks were flushed and pretty and she had the look of a woman who is in love. I felt shut out from it. I felt a little dismayed. There she was looking the best I had seen her look for ages and it was nothing to do with me. For a moment I was cross with myself for feeling like this. After all, we do not own people; we cannot own them. What is monogamy but a desire to possess somebody completely? Even their beauty has to be yours. That night her beauty felt such a private thing; it was between her and her love. I felt I was interrupting things even to notice it as fully as I did. I too was wearing a new dress.Our friends arrived and everybody was sitting talking and drinking quite merrily when Isadora walked into the room. I didn't think her so very beautiful but as soon as she walked in I saw Anna's eyes light up and her cheeks grow even more flushed. I decided I had to take control of the situation by being very friendly towards Isadora. I said, Isadora how lovely to meet you at last, I have heard so much about you. Anna has really been enjoying playing with you. She is so excited about this concert that you are going to be doing. Isadora was friendly back to me, but a little uncomfortable. She looked as if she had made the wrong decision and actually wanted to be somewhere else. She nodded and said she too was looking forward and then she looked around the room as if asking for help.

After the food and the wine, we went into the room with the baby grand piano and Isadora started tuning her violin. She looked so concentrated as she did it, even slightly bad-tempered. I noticed her arms looked strong. I noticed she had a bruise under her chin where her violin rested, quite a dark bruise the size of a plum. I noticed the beautiful colour of her violin, a rich orange-blossom wood. Anna sat down at the piano and together they started to play the sonata. The room filled with the sound of their music. They smiled at each other as they were playing like two people that were passing some important, some crucial, some life-or-death secret between them. Like two people that had always known each other, since they were small girls. Like two people who would know each other when they were old women. I was powerless in front of the spectacle of their love. I felt sick to watch it and at the same time kept this composed smile on my face. My face tilted to the side in appreciation of their high art. They played the piece to the end. All the time the music was playing it took me to unbearable places: I forgot myself, then remembered myself, then forgot again. I felt the music strip me of everything I ever owned, everything I ever loved. Outside the sky darkened and it started to rain. The sound of the stormy rain mixed with their music, made it even more intense. And all of a sudden, I felt so alone, so completely alone in a room full of admiring people. I wondered if our friends could see what I could see – that Isadora and Anna were meant for each other.

After the piece had finished, I went to my bathroom and stared at myself in the mirror. I felt like I was climbing down the stairs of my love, and that when I got to the bottom I would be lost. I could no longer tell myself that I was imagining things. It was plain to me. Now all I had to do was decide what to do and when to leave. And if I had just simply enjoyed the concert and congratulated them and allowed them to enjoy this time together, it would have all been very different, for me at least.

It is very dark now and your voice has become very low like the lowering dark. It has become one with the land outside the window, mysterious and untouchable, and remote. And because it is so remote it is the most intimate sound I have ever heard. I want to stop you now. I want to say, Whatever you did, I forgive you. Don't tire yourself out telling me any more now. Let us just enjoy this journey in the dark together. Let us have no more words. Your face is in shadows. You are hunched up into yourself. I can barely make you out. The train stops at another station. We have only one hour before we reach our destination. My mind is racing, trying to think ahead to how you might have ended things. I don't imagine you feel anything for me very much. But I have noticed the way you move your hands when you talk, the way you push some strands of your hair away from your face, the way you cross and uncross your legs. In this carriage with you, I could continue, across our troubled country for a very long time. I would like to pull a blanket down from above and wrap it around your lovely shoulders and tuck you up. Then I

would like to kiss your cheek. And I would like
to be bold enough to say, It is as well all this
happened because you were meant to meet me
and I would never betray you. I love the sound
of your voice. I love the way you close your
eyes when you are trying to think of a word. I
love the way you tell a story. Could you, perhaps, love somebody like me? Somebody who
has no grace, who is big-boned and clumsy, but
somebody who appreciates every fine thing in
life and will give you only fine things ever and
will only ever treat you as you deserve to be
treated? I can see that you are a woman of
delicate tastes.

You close your eyes for a moment. I can tell
you are getting to the difficult bit of your story.
I am not sure I want to hear it. You are still perfect to me. Everything you have said so far I
can understand. I am still with you. I don't
want you to say something that will make me
part company with you. I don't want you to be

crazy. I feel as if I have known you for a very long time.

But there is nothing I can do to stop you. You sigh and tears roll down your cheeks and you say to me simply, tired of the details, I couldn't take any more. When Isadora left that night I confronted my Anna. I said to her, It was so obvious that you love her. I am sure everybody in the room saw. Why won't you simply be honest with me and tell me the truth? She stared at me very surprised and she said, You make up so much in your head. I don't know you any more, Esther. I want us to separate. I can't live with this kind of suspicion. It is killing me. It has already killed us. You have made yourself up this long and elaborate story because you have fallen out of love with me. I gave out an incredulous gasp at this point. Yes, she said, it is you who have tired of me. You are simply needing me to do it. Very well. I will break it off. Enough. Enough, Esther! I have had enough! And she picked up a paperweight and hurled it across the room. It narrowly missed me. I ran at her and grabbed her by her shoulders and screamed at her, How dare you make me think I am going mad when you know very well you love her. How dare you? I slapped her straight across the face. I felt thrilled to be at last able to act decisively. I whipped myself up into a state of absolute dejected fury and it felt better than the lonely quiet times I had had. So much better. I slapped her again. I said to her coldly, I hate you. Get out. Get out of my life. She went to our bedroom and pulled down the suitcase from the top of the wardrobe and started packing. She was crying more out of indignation than anything else. I would never have believed this of you, Esther, she said. That you could act so crazy. I am not safe around you. I never meant to hurt you. I only ever meant to love you. Who knows where it goes to, this love, when it goes?

Who knows where it goes? She said this sadly, to herself, shaking her head. She was packing quickly as she spoke. It was the most open she had spoken to me for months. I was startled for a moment then the rage came back even worse. I looked at the back of her head and hated the shape of it.

So you admit it has gone after all, I said nastily. You have made it go, she said. You and your crazy jealousy and your imaginings. Isadora would never go with a woman. She is happily married with two children.

She looked so self-righteous when she said this, as if nobody had ever heard of a married woman going off with another woman.

Well, she packed up and she left that night. I ripped the curtains off the windows and threw them out into the street as she got in a taxi. I screamed, Take these. They are your curtains. But of course she didn't take them.

All night that night, anybody could have

stared into my apartment. She looked up at me and she waved and I will never forget that wave of hers as long as I live. Three months later she was dead. I never saw her again.

I sit forward in my seat. I am alarmed. I had not expected the story to finish like this and I am devastated. What do you mean, dead, I say like an idiot.

I am tired speaking in English, you say. My own language is mixing up with it and I am exhausted. Too many sounds in my head.

Yes, but what do you mean dead, I say again. What do you mean? How did she die?

You speak very slowly, thickly, as if there is fur in your mouth. Your voice is flat. I imagine you outside the train wading through the deep, thick snow, alone. You are so cold. You are shivering. I cannot believe she is dead.

She had cancer. She had a very fast cancer that swept through her body and took her very quickly. She never told me. Nobody did. She didn't want to see me again. Then a couple of days before she died, I got a card from her, that told me nothing about her being ill but simply asked if I would come and visit her in her new place. I wrote back saying should I expect to see Isadora there too? And a few days after that I got a call from a mutual friend that told me Anna was dead.

And it was too late for me. It was too late for my jealousy. It was too late for everything. You cannot turn the clock back when somebody dies. You are consigned to always turning it forward and to seeing the bleak years stretch out ahead of you like the snow thinking if only, if only, if only. The future is endless when someone dies; you have years and years of not them, years to get through your life as best as you can. And what does it all matter, those petty jealousies compared to a life, to a love, what does it matter? Jealousy is as cruel and as cold as the snow. It bites, it takes you out, it gets you lost. You can never return from jealousy. Once you have gone there, you cannot get back. You cannot come back the same way.

I try and comfort you for you are really crying now. Well, I say, you weren't to know. I go over to your side of the carriage and put my arm around you. I hold you tightly. I say, There, there, hush, but you weren't to know, hush, hush, hush. All you did was love too fiercely.

And now I think, maybe she could feel it, this illness inside her. Maybe that was the passion. Maybe the passion was death, the passion was that she had to play that one piece of music brilliantly before she died and I spoiled it. I will never, ever be able to forgive myself. Never. I loved her. I will never love again like that. And she never got to play in that concert with Isadora. She died a few days before the concert was supposed to happen.

You sob now, out loud on the train. The

guard walks by outside in the corridor and stops for a second, listens, then walks on. 'I might as well have killed her.'

I forgive you, I say. I forgive you. I recite some Latin remembered from school days. In nomino nomina nominas padre, madre, some nonsense cobbled up but soothing sounding, padre, madre, nomino nomina, dulce et decorum est pro patria mori. I have reverted to war poetry now. You hold both my cheeks in your hands and through your tears you say, Thank you, thank you, and you kiss the tears from my face and then you kiss my lips briefly. You take off my green scarf and go to hand it back to me. Keep it, I say to you. Please, I would like you to have it.

You wrap it around your beautiful neck.

And then our train reaches its destination. I have been dreading it would get there and knowing that it would, knowing that arrival was inevitable, unavoidable. How bizarre, I think to myself, to be on a train and to actually not want to arrive anywhere? What kind of madness is that? I get your suitcase down from the luggage rack and I pull my small bag down as well. I climb down the steep steps of the train then I help you down too. You seem weak from all your talking.

We walk along the platform very slowly together, like people that have suddenly become old together on the course of a single journey. We walk side by side in silence. I don't know if you dread parting like I do. You have stopped talking altogether. We pass through the station. I imagine what we look like from above. Two trusting people with their luggage walking slowly through the station after a long, long journey. I think of asking you for your address, for your phone number. I think of saying, It would be so lovely to keep in touch, would it not. I try and pluck up the courage to say this one simple sentence as we wait together in the taxi queue.

I think about how lonely Anna would have felt dying without her love. I think about why she didn't contact you sooner. I think about pride, how pride distorts and demeans. It is freezing cold. The temperature must be minus fifteen. The air crackles. The skin on my face tightens. The taxi queue grows inevitably shorter and we reach the front too fast. Again I have the terrible feeling of not wanting to get to the front of the queue, not wanting to leave you. You look round at me for a second as though you are going to say something. And all of a sudden you are climbing into your taxi and I am holding your door open before I get into mine. All of a sudden I am opening the door of my taxi and suppressing the desire to simply say, Follow that taxi. I don't know what to do with myself. I sit as close as I can to the window.

Sonata

Our taxis travel together up the steep short road from the station. We stop at a red traffic light together. I am looking into the back of your taxi. I have no idea where it is heading for. Then it happens, the thing happens, your taxi turns to the left and mine turns to the right and I turn round frantically and wave at you out of the back window and you wave at me swivelling round too. I can see my green scarf wrapped round your lovely neck. You keep your hand pressed to the back window of your taxi. I take my hand and press it to the window of mine. Our hands are like our train stopped at the station.

PICADOR SHOTS

SHALOM AUSLANDER
'Holocaust Tips for Kids' and 'Smite the Heathens,
Charlie Brown' from *Beware of God*

CRAIG DAVIDSON
'A Mean Utility' and 'Life in the Flesh' from *Rust and Bone*

BRET EASTON ELLIS
'Water from the Sun' and 'Discovering Japan'
from *The Informers*

NELL FREUDENBERGER
'Lucky Girls' from *Lucky Girls*

ALEKSANDAR HEMON
'Exchange of Pleasant Words' and 'A Coin'
from *The Question of Bruno*

JACKIE KAY
'Sonata' from *Wish I Was Here*

MATTHEW KNEALE
'Powder' from *Small Crimes in An Age of Abundance*

CLAIRE MESSUD
'The Professor's History'

JAMES SALTER
'My Lord You' and 'Palm Court' from *Last Night*

COLM TÓIBÍN
'The Use of Reason' from *Mothers and Sons*

NIALL WILLIAMS
unpublished new story – 'The Unrequited'

TIM WINTON
'Small Mercies' from *The Turning*

All collections are available in Picador.